THE ESCAPE OF HANNA SCHMIDT

and other

stories and poems

selected by
Stewart Ross

An anthology of winning stories from the 2009-2010
World Book Day Short Stories competition

KT-492-463

In association

NATE

Published in 2010 by Evans Brothers Limited
2A Portman Mansions
Chiltern Street
London W1U 6NR

British Library Cataloguing in Publication Data
A catalogue record for this book is available from
the British Library

ISBN: 9780237541293

Editor: Bryony Jones
Designers:
Rebecca Fox, Evans
Jo Kennedy, Us2Design

Foreword

Three years ago, when I first selected stories for this book, I was amazed at the quality of the entries. Not any more. I now know, from past experience and from visiting dozens of schools all over Britain and further afield, that the pool of secondary school talent is deep, wide and wonderfully rich. And if you think I'm saying that just to be polite, skip this foreword and start reading the stories and poems themselves….

The World Book Day / Evans Short Stories Competition goes from strength to strength. This year we had more entries than ever and the standard keeps climbing. I offer all who entered, especially those whose work is included here, my most sincere congratulations.

As in previous years, it has not been possible to print as many entries as we would have wished. We began the selection process by making a shortlist of 60 from the submissions in the over-11 age group. I then had the unenviable task of selecting two or three pieces beginning with each of the six opening lines, producing the final 13 printed here.

The stories included are by no means the 'best'. That would be an impossible claim. Writing and reading are very personal experiences, so the writing in this book is simply my selection, the entries I liked best. I have also tried to offer a cross-section of ages and regions.

How did I make my choice? Obviously all shortlisted entries stuck to the rules and were well enough punctuated for me to understand what they were trying to say. (I confess to being a bit of a stickler for punctuation: clear punctuation usually shows that a writer is thinking of the reader as they write.) After that I went for originality, fresh and exciting language, and short stories as opposed to mini-novels.

One piece of advice? Unless you are keeping a diary, you are writing for the reader. Think of them, make it fun for them and make it easy for them, especially by cutting down those monster paragraphs.

Thank you for sharing your talent with me and well done, everyone.

Stewart Ross
Blean, 2010

Acknowledgements

The 2009-2010 World Book Day Short Stories Competition has seen more schools registering and more entries than ever before. A huge thank you to every teacher and librarian for encouraging their students to enter and to every student for writing or illustrating a story or poem.

The entries we received were of an exceptional standard, with winners across the two age categories ranging from five to 17 years old. The new poetry aspect of the competition really captured students' imaginations and helped the competition to grow and continue to go from strength to strength.

Congratulations to the worthy winners and commiserations to those that didn't win. Don't lose heart, remember that even the most successful authors weren't published on their first attempt. We appreciate the hard work and creative effort that goes into every student's entry.

A special thank you is due to all the authors who provided opening lines, and to their publishers. And to Stewart Ross, who once again took on the difficult and unenviable role of judging the competition, and without whom this competition would be an impossible task.

For all their hard work in helping to organise the competition, thanks go to Cathy Schofield of

World Book Day, Truda Spruyt of Colman Getty and Jo Kennedy of US2 for the fantastic cover designs.

Keep an eye on www.worldbookday.com and www.evansbooks.co.uk for information about the next World Book Day Short Stories Competition.

Thanks
Evans Books

Contents

'From the other side of the wall, I could hear their footsteps getting closer. It was definitely now or never.'

Andy McNab

Home Sweet Home

by Ben Turner

From the other side of the wall, I could hear their footsteps getting closer. It was definitely now or never. Beads of sweat were running down my face in the cold night and fear clung to me like a predator grips its prey. My younger brother, Timothy, was trembling beside me, his small face as pale as the moon. We made a break for it and sprinted away from the sprawling, sinister building in which we had been held, towards the dark woods. But we didn't go unnoticed. We could hear angry voices. 'Over there, towards the woods!' they shouted.

We needed to find somewhere to hide and fast. Timothy's legs buckled beneath him. I grabbed his small, bony hand and pleaded with him to get up. 'Come on Tim, we've got to get away, don't give up!' We cowered in the damp, dense shrubbery of the woods, our feet sinking into the cold, sticky mud. I could not bear the thought of what would happen to us if we were caught....

The forest seemed to come alive in the darkness, with the occasional hoot of an owl and the rustling of leaves in the night breeze. With the moon disappearing behind the clouds even the most familiar noises sounded ominous. Timothy was whimpering beside me, clutching my hand so tightly that a sharp pain ran constantly along my arm. I daren't let go for fear of Tim crying out and giving away our hiding place. The footsteps were getting even closer now, the regular thudding of feet sending tremors throughout my body. *Please don't let them find us,* I prayed silently. As quietly as possible, I urged my body further down into the damp undergrowth, willing their footsteps to pass by. I could barely breathe, my chest tightening with pure terror. Was this what it felt like before you died? Timothy was huddled tightly against me – I had never felt so responsible for him in my entire life.

Their footsteps were getting closer, their torches flooding the clearing around us with light, highlighting the eerie outline of the trees. I dared not move for fear of attracting attention, my heart pounding. To my relief, the thud of footsteps was gradually getting fainter and fainter. I daren't let myself believe that we were finally safe. I decided that we should stay put until morning, just to be sure. Tim dozed off beside me, snuggled into my body like a caterpillar in its cocoon. I almost felt jealous looking down at him – he had me to look after him... I was so cold, hungry and lonely. The slightest noise from the forest would make my body jerk, causing Tim to stir beside me. I had to come up with a plan. We couldn't run the risk of being caught. I yearned to be back with my parents, in the safety and comfort of my home. They were going to be so desperately overjoyed to see us....

We stayed in our hiding place until dawn broke, the orange glare of sunrise illuminating the morning sky. The call of the birds produced a cacophony of noise. We awoke shivering, our bodies cramped and sore. We rose slowly from our hiding place and checked that no one was around before making our way tentatively through the woods. After some time, we eventually found a train station. We sat down heavily on the station bench to catch our breath, all the while glancing warily around to make sure no one was following. In the distance we were relieved to see the approaching lights of a train. When it finally pulled in, we jumped on quickly and locked ourselves in the nearest toilet in case a ticket inspector was on board. When the train finally arrived in central London, I felt relieved that we were almost home. The only way to get our tube fare though, to travel home to north London, was to beg for money, something I had never done before. Thankfully, people took pity on us – our dirty and dishevelled clothes, together with Tim's sickly pallor, meant that we soon had enough money for our fare home.

With our tickets clutched tightly in our hands, we boarded the tube to Camden, becoming increasingly excited at the thought of seeing our parents once more. Walking along Camden High Street, a policeman eyed us suspiciously, so we darted into the market to hide. My heart was pounding. The policeman's search ended as abruptly as it started.

As we turned off the High Street into our street we started walking faster, forgetting our aching limbs. We finally stood before our front door, finding comfort in its familiarity. It was breakfast time and I could smell bacon and eggs and hear Radio 4 blaring from the kitchen. My stomach lurched and my body ached with hunger. I rang the doorbell and waited impatiently for Mum or Dad to answer. Mum opened the door and paled instantly with shock, tears springing to her eyes.

'Mum what's wrong?' I asked. 'It's me, George.'

'Come here, quick!' she shouted tearfully to my father, her voice trembling.

I could hear Dad thundering down the stairs, two at a time. When he reached the front door and saw us standing there, his eyes seemed to bulge and his face went red with rage. He looked as mad as could be. Pulling us in the house by the scruff of our necks, he yelled, 'Get in here now!', glancing up and down the street as he did so. We stumbled into the house, confused and bewildered. Wasn't he pleased to have us back home? He shoved us aggressively into the cupboard under the stairs, locking it us behind us. Tim and I peered at each other in the dark, clutching hands, terrified once more. We could hear Dad making a phone call.

'What's happening?' Tim whimpered.

'Is that the children's home?' Dad barked. 'What kind of place do you think you're running there? My two kids, George and Timothy Smith have run away and turned up here at home! I told you before, we don't want them, never did. I want one of your people over here *right now* to pick them up – and make it quick....'

Ben Turner, aged 11
British Section Lycée International, Paris, France

The Escape of Hanna Schmidt

by Grace Ann Jalleh-Sharples

From the other side of the wall, I could hear their footsteps getting closer. It was definitely now or never. I had stood silent in the shadows for an hour, counting, watching, barely daring to breathe. Fourteen seconds for the searchlights to sweep from right to left, like the fingers of a blind man reaching into the dark. Forty-five seconds for the guards to walk between the watchtowers. I would have 12 seconds to cross the minefield. Instinctively I fingered the breast pocket of my tired, shapeless coat, checking the document was still there. How is it that I, Hanna Schmidt, a 22-year-old secretary in the Ministry of Home Affairs, was about to escape over the Berlin Wall?

'Hanna, what are you doing, you silly little thing?' The bundle of papers I had been sent to copy had fluttered to the office floor. I was bent double picking them up frantically.

'I am so sorry, Herr Kreutzman!' I said as I gathered the last few sheets. Fortunately he didn't notice there was an extra set for my 'friends' on the other side of the wall. I thought it would be harder. No one noticed or paid much attention to this dowdy worker bee.

'Poor thing,' said Herr Kreutzman to Herr Gruber as I hurried away, almost dropping the papers again. 'Nothing really to recommend her, is there?'

I had been doing this for a year – giving information to the other side. Nothing really important. Just facts and figures: crop reports, tractor production figures, and so on. No military secrets – I had scruples. Berlin in the 1960s was full of spies. Half of the people seemed to be spying on the other half or each other. In every bar and café and on every street corner there was someone pointing a hidden camera or microphone.

Some did it for money. Some did it for the glamour or out of boredom. You may find it surprising but some, like me, did it out of principle. For as long as I could remember, I had dreamed of living on the other side of the wall, where I would be valued, appreciated. I hated my country, what it stood for, what it did to people. What it made them become. I wanted to live somewhere where people were happy and free.

My childhood had been routine, even normal, I suppose. My parents had just survived the war but that had taken all they had. They were older than their years and exhausted. As time went by, they paid me less and less attention. Death took them quickly, one shortly after the other, with little struggle. I could fit their life into two suitcases.

I had no family and no longer any reason to stay. I could remember nothing of the war. The wall, though, had always been there as long as I could remember. Separating Us from Them. Always in my mind. Always in view or just around the corner. We all lived in its shadow. I had been a below-average student. Not someone you'd remember. Just one of the ones who pass through without leaving a mark. I had no friends, no real friends. You didn't know who you could trust.

I had worked in the ministry since I was 16. I suppose, then, I was ready for him. It was Hans, you see, who got me into this. We met in the staff canteen and he started to sit near me. He had an easy smile and a gentle laugh. It was nice to have someone pay some attention. He said it was the right thing to do. He said I'd be helping both sides understand each other. I suppose I wanted to believe.

I was surprised how easy it was. I half expected a heavy hand on my shoulder the first time I walked down the steps of the ministry with the papers tucked into my shirt. No one stopped me. No one searched me. I got home with my heart hammering in my chest, gulping air. Over time it became normal, routine even.

But rumours started to spread. Difficult questions were being asked. Everyone knew there was a leak. The person had to be found.

The border crossings had been closed to prevent escape.

In my office people gathered in small groups, muttering under their breath and staring suspiciously at others. The police were interviewing everyone. Typically German, they started at 'A' and worked through the alphabet. Lucky for Schmidt.

Yet I knew that eventually they would come for me. I had to leave. One last set of papers. The ones now in my coat pocket I was fingering nervously as I stood by the wall. Cowering. Waiting for the searchlight to pass. Hiding from the guards. Praying my scent would be carried away from their Alsatians' twitching noses. The icy wind whipped through my thin layers and I shivered violently. I could stay no more.

As the searchlight passed, I broke cover and started to run across no-man's land, praying I wouldn't step on one of the landmines. Frantically. Silently. The worst game of hopscotch in the world.

'One, two, three...' I muttered through gritted teeth as I stumbled across the uneven ground. In the distance I could hear sounds of normality: a stray dog barking, a scream. How had they not noticed me? Were they all asleep? Was this all a joke?

'Four, five, six....' The searchlight had now come to the end of its arc and was starting its way back towards me. Would the guards on the other side take me as a friend or foe? 'Seven, eight....'

'HALT!' screamed a voice from one of the watchtowers. 'OVER THERE.' The searchlight spun and caught me in its beam, like a butterfly specimen pinned to a board. I broke into a staggering run. My heel tore off. No time to think about mines now.

'HALT!' cried the voice again.

'Nine, ten….' I heard the crackle of automatic gunfire from behind. The ground spat up either side of me. I was sure a bullet would thump into my back and I would fall lifeless to the ground.

'Eleven, twelve….' I clawed desperately at the grey concrete of the other wall, my lungs screaming in agony. A metal door opened noisily. Two guards in slate-grey uniforms with guns stood behind it.

'Welcome to East Berlin, Fraulein.'

Grace Ann Jalleh-Sharples, aged 13
Clifton College, Bristol

'When my dad sat me down and told me he had something important to share with me, the last thing I expected to hear was, "You're a vampire." '

Justin Somper

A Vampire's Dress

by Rose Proudfoot

**When my dad sat me down and told me he had
something important to share with me, the last
thing I expected to hear was, 'You're a vampire.'**
I laughed at the idea of it. How utterly ridiculous.
He knew that 'vampire' was never going to
happen. I looked at him and giggled. He was
giving me a really serious look, but behind his
deep grey eyes I could see the twinkle of laughter
I loved. There was another second of silence
and then we both exploded into loud peals of
helpless laughter.

After I had composed myself, I reached
for the hideous vampire costume my dad was
holding and examined it closely. It was awful.
Black string cobwebs clung to the puffy arms
and it cackled when you pressed a button on
the shoulder. It was full length and completely
shapeless. The whole thing screamed tack! I gave
a half-disgusted, half-amused snort, and returned
the monstrosity to the rail.

'No Dad, never in a million years am I going
to be seen wearing that!'

The invitation had clearly said fancy dress.

Not 'Come in the worst item of clothing you can possibly find'!

'I've told you! I want something mature and sophisticated, not something that's going to make me look like a member of the Adams family!' My voice was serious, but I was smiling. My dad always tried to understand what I saw as good and bad (clothes wise), but unfortunately, his lack of fashion sense for himself made it impossible for him to help me choose anything halfway decent in a clothes shop. But he still came, to make up for Mum not being there. He always felt so guilty for her leaving. Not that it was his fault that she went off and had an affair.

We started over to a section of the costume shop called 'Elegance'. Sounded promising. I walked quickly through 'Comedy', a section filled with clown costumes. Hilarious… not. I hated clowns, had done ever since I was a toddler. Mum had taken me to a travelling circus, I'd laughed at all the acts, the fire-eaters, the trapeze artists, but then a bunch of clowns came running through the audience, laughing in people's faces. I was terrified! One clown came up to me and started trying to cheer me up, but that just made things worse. I had started to scream and cry in panic. Clowns are not my favourite things, at all!

I reached 'Elegance' and gasped. Yes! It was perfect! There, modelled on a painfully thin mannequin, was the dress of my dreams! It was one of those old ones, like you see in Jane Austen films. It was a light powdery blue and was covered in delicate white lace. Stunning is the only way I can describe it, I had fallen in love. After a minute of gazing at the dress, I ran to the rails, searching. It had to be there somewhere. Casting aside dress after dress, I continued my frantic search. Then I saw it. Bliss! Checking the size, I took it from the rail. Perfect, size 12, it should fit fine. Dad arrived by my side and said, 'That's rather nice, isn't it?'

'Yes,' I replied happily, 'it's perfect!'

'How much?' asked Dad curiously.

Oh no! In the sheer wonderfulness of the moment I hadn't even thought about the price. Hesitantly I checked the label. Bloody hell! It was 80 pounds! There was no way on earth Dad would let me get it for 80 pounds! I signed heavily. 'Eighty,' I replied gloomily.

'Hmmm, well I suppose I could….'

I was thrilled, my heartbeat doubled and I grinned uncontrollably. My dad was actually going to buy me the dress of my dreams. This party was going to be sooo….

'Wait a minute hun, let's see that label. What! You have to be joking! I thought you said 18, not 80! There is no way I'm paying 80 pounds for that!'

The night was cold and I shivered as I walked up the front steps of the house towards the door. I could hear the muffled sound of music coming from inside, and lights were flashing at the windows. I felt sick. I couldn't believe my dad had actually talked me into this. Here I was, standing outside of the party of the year, in a hideous vampire dress. The humiliation! Knowing I had to go in at some point, I groaned and opened the door.

The music was almost deafeningly loud and yet somehow everyone in the room had heard me come in. Thirty heads turned in my direction and then stared at me with looks of shock and amusement on their faces. I wanted to crawl into a hole and die! I was completely and utterly humiliated.

Scanning the room, I could see that the vast majority of girls were in beautiful dresses (but none quite as beautiful as the lacy blue one in the shop). Even the few who weren't in dresses were other very feminine things such as fairies and flowers. The boys' costumes varied. There was a gorilla, a giant bear and Yoda, to name a few, and all were staring silently at me. The silence was awful. I prayed something would break it. Even the music had stopped. That's when it happened. There was a completely disastrous technical malfunction in the dress, and it began its cackily mechanical cackle, over and over again. I wanted to run. Perhaps nobody had recognised me. I could still make it out if....

There he was, over on the other side of the room, smiling right at me, but not in a nasty way. In a completely wonderful way. He was gorgeous, he was perfect, he was... coming towards me!!

Oh no. How could I possibly talk to this lad in the state I was in!? In the clothes I was in!? It was completely, awfully disastrous. Oh God! He was getting closer. Thankfully some people had begun to talk again. Probably about me, but that was the least of my worries. He had almost reached me. I felt like fainting!

That was when I realised he was wearing a vampire costume. We were both wearing vampire costumes. It was too good to be true! I hit my shoulder where the cackle button was, it hurt but the cackling stopped.

'Hi,' he said casually. I immediately loved his voice.

'Hiya,' I croaked back, gazing dreamily into his big green eyes.

'I love your costume, it's so individual, unlike all these sheep,' he said, gesturing towards the crowd of girls in front of me. 'My name's Matt.'

'Hi Matt,' I grinned, 'I'm very pleased to meet you!' Thank God I came as a vampire!!

I guess Dad does know what he's talking about some of the time!

Rose Proudfoot, aged 13
The County High School, Leftwich, Cheshire

A Birthday Surprise

by Jake Billings

When my dad sat me down and told me he had something important to share with me, the last thing I expected to hear was, 'You're a vampire.' I swallowed hard. What was wrong with my dad? Was he having a breakdown, I wondered? How could I possibly be a vampire, I didn't have pointy teeth, I couldn't stand the sight of blood never mind the taste of it. I could go out in daylight and I could see my reflection in the mirror. I looked at Dad, and expected him to start laughing, but he didn't. His face was deadly serious. I just couldn't get my head around the news, and why did he wait to tell me until the night before my thirteenth birthday?

A long, long time ago, a count called Dracula had put a curse on one of my ancestors. He had worked for the count as a servant in his castle and he had fallen in love with Dracula's daughter, and wanted to marry her. Count Dracula wouldn't let this happen, so they ran away together and he cursed them both and all of their children for future generations.

I still didn't get why Dad had waited almost 13 years to tell me this story. Then he dropped the bombshell! Thirteen was the number of evil and it was certainly going to be unlucky for me tomorrow! Tomorrow I would become a proper vampire, just like my dad, my granddad, my great granddad and my great, great granddad, etc did on their thirteenth birthdays. My dad and granddads all seemed to cope well with being vampires. Maybe I would too. After all I never knew the family secret until today.

I nervously went to bed that night, not knowing what I was going to wake up like the next morning. Just before he went to work, my dad came into my bedroom and told me not to worry too much, everything would be cool. I lay awake for ages, thinking. My dad had always worked nights for as long as I could remember and whenever it was hot and sunny he dressed as though it was winter. He never wore shorts or t-shirts, but he'd always wear his dark sunglasses. We used to laugh at him and call him weird. As I lay there a terrible thought crossed my mind. Was Dad really working nights in the factory? Or was he really out hunting for blood? Was being a vampire the same as in the horror films?

After a surprisingly good night's sleep I woke up early. Yes! I was a teenager today. No! I was also a vampire today. I ran into the bathroom, looked in the mirror and saw my reflection staring back. How could I be a vampire when I could still see myself in the mirror? Perhaps I had escaped the curse or maybe it had been a dream. I grinned. It was then that I caught sight of my two enormous, gleaming white fangs. I screamed! Dad had just got home from work. He came running into the bathroom, Mum's nail file in his hand. Before I could ask what the nail file was for, he started filing the ends off my fangs to make them straight again and told me I must do this every week, so that no one would guess my secret.

I put my school uniform on and ran downstairs to open my birthday cards and presents. The first one that I opened was my very own nail/tooth file, then came the special 500 factor sun cream from Mum and Dad, which I was supposed to wear every time I went out in the daylight from now on. That was fine, but where was the Nintendo DS that I'd asked for? My presents grew increasingly strange as I opened them. There was a vampire manual from my great grandparents, which explained how to turn into a bat and how to move at lightning speed. There was a long, black cape and a pair of really dark designer sunglasses off my grandparents. At last I opened my Nintendo DS and a new game. This might not be such an unlucky birthday after all!

At eight-thirty my friend called for me to go to school. He was impressed with my new sunglasses and thought they were cool. He wanted a pair for his birthday. I slipped my manual into my school bag and we set off to catch the bus. It wouldn't hurt to look through it. I wouldn't mind being as fast as lightning. I had a great day at school and everything went as normal. I decided to walk home instead of catching the bus with my friends.

On the way home I began collecting dandelion stalks, because according to the manual if you suck the juice from five dandelion stems you can do everything at supersonic speed. I went straight up to my room when I got in, and took a deep breath before sucking my first dandelion stem. It was absolutely disgusting and it made me feel sick, but if I wanted to do things at super speed, then I had to be brave. I held my nose and sucked the other four stems. I didn't feel any different at all. What a load of rubbish that book was!

I'd almost made myself sick for nothing. I got my books out and began to do my homework. My French, Science and English were all due in the next day. This was going to take me ages and I was hoping to play on my Nintendo before bedtime. I was just putting the finishing touches to my English when Mum called me down to tea. I looked at my watch and I couldn't believe my eyes, I had finished all three subjects in just three minutes. Wow that juice had certainly worked! Mum kept telling me to slow down while I was eating my food or I'd get indigestion.

After about an hour the effects of the dandelion juice began to wear off and I was back to normal – well as close to normal as I could be now.

I got up really early the next morning, checked to see if my fangs needed filing, rubbed on my sun cream, put on my designer sunglasses and went out to pick some more dandelions. Today I had decided that I was going to try out for the school footy team and athletics team, and when I'd taken my supersonic juice, Mr Marshall the P.E. teacher would be begging me to play for the school. I'd be one of the most popular kids in school, instead of the one that nobody ever noticed.

Dad was right when he told me everything would be cool. Not only was it cool being a vampire, it was ACE!

Jake Billings, aged 12
Tower House School, Torbay, Devon

'I don't know whose fault
she thought it was, but it
definitely wasn't mine.'

Linda Newbery

Through the eyes of Wilfred

by April La

I don't know whose fault she thought it was, but it definitely wasn't mine. Shards of glass scattered the cage floor, the woman infuriated as I cowered in the corner. I didn't mean to bite her but she frightened me. Let me tell you my story from the beginning so you'll understand....

The Outside
One year I'd lived in here behind rusty metal bars, the smell of damp hay wafted in the room, if it wasn't the aroma of rotten vegetables fed to us once a day. Not much sunlight penetrated the wooden walls but we didn't mind the darkness. There were hundreds of us living here; I lived with a female, called Pippy. Conversations were always about one thing: the outside. We shared our ideas, some believable but none of us had seen it... yet.

Later in the day the worker cleaned our room but left shortly, letting us back in. Nothing new ever happened apart from some of my acquaintances were taken away.

41

The last of the workers locked up for the night and Pippy had fallen asleep. I was drinking water when I noticed our door. It was moving forward and back very slightly. I nudged it gently with my nose. It creaked open and I nudged it again. My nose twitched in curiosity and I slowly stepped out. I'd never been out of my room before when the idea popped into my head. If I found an exit I could go… outside. Adventure was staring me in the face and I couldn't ignore it when I saw a hole at the bottom of the wall panel. I scurried to the opportunity, easily fitting through and as I emerged it was extraordinary. The ground was green and there were tall figures swaying in the silent breeze. Looking up was magical, for it was a sea of deep blue and twinkling lights. The outside was so alien but beautiful. I spotted a red object, round and shiny. I nibbled it. So delicious! Sweet, crunchy, it was scrumptious! I'd only been out for a few minutes but I felt so free. Then suddenly two big boots stood in front of me; a towering figure lifted me up. I realised it was the cage cleaner I saw earlier in the day and he placed me back into my room, locking it up. Back inside. I wasn't out long but I'd never felt so free. I only confided in Pippy.

The Unit

Two weeks had passed and Pippy and I were being moved to a place called 'the unit'. I hoped during the movement I could have a glance at the outside, but I was sadly disappointed when they drove the vehicle into the building. Many others were loaded onto the truck as well and the journey began as the door closed.

The door drew open and we were somewhere new; a white building. We were taken to a room and the door read 'Mice room'. As we entered, there were hundreds of cages with mice and I recognised some of the faces. We joined the group and had food and water brought to us.

'Where are we?' I asked Pippy.

'I don't know. I've never seen a place like this before.'

I studied the room but I had no idea.

Three days have gone by and I'm still confused. Obviously this was going to be our new home but I didn't feel comfortable here. It was bright and people kept coming in. As I pondered, our cage door opened. Pippy and I rushed to the back of the cage but a hand grabbed Pippy tightly and pulled her away. She struggled and was taken out. Where was she being taken?

When she was brought back I was petrified. Pink covered her eyes, it was powdery but what was it? She darted to the corner and lay shivering. 'Pippy?' I queried.

'Th… they put something on me… and others,' she stuttered.

'What is that stuff?'

'I don't know but it burns,' she cried in pain.

I could do nothing but watch her in agony. Whatever this place was it was hurting Pippy and probably others. I didn't know much, but one thing I did know was that I was scared.

Goodbye

Next morning Pippy's eyes were swollen up like balloons and she was scratching them.

'Help, I can't see,' she whimpered. I couldn't do anything; I didn't know what was wrong. I was nuzzling her when our cage opened and Pippy was taken out again. They were hurting her and I could do nothing. When she came back she was weaker and stumbled around.

'Did they hurt you again?' I asked, enraged.

'They stuck something sharp in me... it hurt,' she whispered, weak. We slept till morning.

I awoke still aware of Pippy's problems. I nudged her trying to wake her but she did not move. I nudged her harder but nothing. She was cold. She couldn't be... they didn't....

'Pippy... you're just sleeping yeh?' I murmured. No reply. I tried again but nothing. She was gone. They made her go through pain, she never hurt anyone and they killed her. I lay next to her lifeless body and nuzzled her fur. I was alone. A hand drew in and took her away; I tried gripping her but how could I hold on? Pippy was gone.

A few minutes later the woman came back and opened my cage. I scurried to the back but

44

she grabbed me. I remembered Pippy, foreseeing my fate. I sank my teeth into her fingers and she released, hitting my water bottle, shattering it. I don't know whose fault she thought it was, but it definitely wasn't mine. Now we're back to the start of my story. The woman glared at me, infuriated at my attack and swept up the glass. I sat shivering. As she finished, she picked me up again and took me to a room. Mice and other animals were in here with foreign objects applied to them. I know what this place is now. She placed me into a glass box and a man examined me. He held a sharp liquid-filled object close to me; I shut my eyes. But as he almost started a little boy yelled, 'STOP.'

What happened?

'Please don't, Dad, you'll hurt it,' he moaned.

'You shouldn't be here,' he replied sternly.

'I'll keep it, I want to. Please,' he pleaded.

Silence; the man stared at him for a long while then placed me into the boy's hands. 'You best take care of it. It's a boy so don't give it a girl's name,' he approved.

_My_ happy ending

I was taken to his home and a new spacious cage was mine. This boy saved me and gave me a home. His name is Kyle, only nine but he knows how to take care of me. He gave me a name. 'Ok, if you're a boy I think I'll call you… Wilfred. You like that?' he asked, smiling at me.

That is my name, Wilfred. I still go outside

when he plays with me and I always feel free but I still remember Pippy. She never got to see the outside like I did. I wish I could show her. I am safe and cared for with Kyle, but there are the others who are still there. They're tested, suffer and some die. They do not get a happy ending and must bear through the pain. We are considered as emotionless animals, I a vermin, but we feel pain like any other living thing. I wish I could help them but I am only a mouse. I can do nothing, but people like Kyle can make changes and I hope there is a change so they can get their happy ending.

By April La, aged 13
Costello Technology College,
Basingstoke, Hampshire

Understand Me

by Rebecca Jowser

I don't know whose fault she thought it was, but it definitely wasn't mine. It was just a tragic accident, but she was saying I had killed him. I don't understand anything that is going on around me, they are all using such long words. 'Mitigation', 'culpability', what do these words mean? And they all talk so fast, I feel so lost. On and on, psiakóść! – what am I to do? She says 'negligence' and she points at me, stabbing fingers at my heart like she wants to run me through with a skewer. I don't know what this means; I want Serina back. She was nice. The pretty translator lady that helped it all make sense, but now she's gone and they say they won't let her come back. She was not a 'neutral intermediary' – she said more than she should have done. So she is gone. And they all talk so fast and they shout and they argue and they write things down if I don't speak and they write things down when I do speak and… I'm so scared.

Baby Peta and my wife, Maria, sit in the public gallery and they watch with wide eyes. I understand so little, they will understand nothing. They speak no English, we cannot afford the lessons. Enough for me to get a job, then quit. 'Hello sir, good day, excuses me, would you like some tea please?' After lesson five, the book, with its cheerful pictures, had gone, page by page, into the fire, keeping the house warm another night. Page by page, because I had wanted to remember as much as possible. I couldn't read it, but I could recall the pictures: 'Going on the Bus to London' had been about asking for directions, and there had been a big shiny red bus. 'Chatting with Mum' had been about basic conversation, and the picture of the spotty yellow sofa with the stick figures sat on it, taking tea, always tea, had stayed with me, though the letters and words had not. But there had been no pictures for what was happening to me now.

Bare, panelled walls surrounded me, men on either side as I sat in a box with my hands together, chain goes 'clank', 'pobrząkać'. I think I prefer the English. 'Clank'. 'Clinkclank'! I smile. The hammer brings me out of my revive. Bang Bang! Pif Paf! It's starting again.

The angry woman gestures at me, shouts until she cries. I want to know why she is crying, 'Can I help you?' The policeman shushed me, and from the gallery, there are tuts and whispering. That was the wrong thing to say? I keep quiet. The policeman nods, you do that. So I listen hard, piece together the things the barristers are saying, search my sparse mental dictionary, match up words and meanings like a jigsaw. Gradually it starts to come together. Some of things Serina said too, they fit in now. The baby. The baby in the hospital. Very sick. Label writes 'Thomas: Critical. Life Support'. A baby that does not ever cry is a sad thing; just lies there in his little box like a doll. Poor boy, he reminds me of Peta, who is so big and strong compared to this miserable little kitten of a child. I touch the incubator side – he reaches out! Tenderly, I put my hand inside and his tiny hand clasps my fingertip. Then there is a big problem. Doctor comes in, all big noises and anger. 'Hand out incubator very quickly, go back to mopping floors!'

Flustered, I turn around. 'Sorry, sorry. I clean.'

He replies, 'Yes, you bloody well do.' Then he turns and goes back out. All embarrassed, I quickly take the plug out of the wall, plug in the vacuum cleaner, the Hoover, such a nice word! Hooooover! Hoover. Then I remove the plug and leave the ward. I say goodbye to Thomas, 'To be hoping you get better well soon!'

I am dusting the flowers in paediatrics when the angry woman comes and slaps me around the face. She said I killed Thomas with the Hoover! I laugh, this is funny joke?! Sucking up a child with a Hoover? Silly idea! But she is not laughing, and suddenly I realise what says. Hospital equipments need electricity. So do Hoovers. She is crying now, kneeling on the floor, beating her head against the floor until there is blood, but then not stopping. I have done a terrible thing.

I spend many days in the courtroom, all wooden panels and black and white ghosts with their wigs and their gowns, and many nights in the cold, bare cell that had become my home. I think a lot, of Thomas and Peta. Of me. I am a simple man, I want little in my life except to be the architect of a better future for my son than the one he would have got back home. I never meant to hurt anybody or to do anything wrong. Sometimes I cry, other times I pray.

I think Thomas is with God, safe and happy in Heaven away from the worry and pain of his short life. I wish I could tell his mother that he is OK now, and that I am sorry, but the policemen and the officials won't let me. Something about 'jeopardising the trial'. What is 'jeopardising'? I ask for a Polish/English dictionary. They laugh hard and long, then walk out, door slams shut and the key turns in the lock. Clank. Clinkclank. This time I don't smile.

Days turn into weeks into months. So long, but then, all over. Sit down, stand up, sit down, people shouting, then, all quiet. I stand, they sit, they watch, silently. I look around for Peta and Maria, where are they? I can't see them, why are they not here? I don't listen to the judge. He speaks, I look round and round for my family. Then we are leaving, pulled roughly down steps. Not good.

But then, all change. The handcuffs come off, clinkclank. Maria is there. She is smiling but there are tears rolling like winter snows down her pretty face. Instinctively, I put my arms around her, what is wrong? She sobs helplessly into my neck, clutching at me frenziedly. I ask her again, what is wrong? But she only repeats, 'It's all over, all over. Come home. He said you are 'aquitted'. It's all over; it wasn't your fault, just an accident. You can come home.'

And finally I understood.

Rebecca Jowser, aged 16
Haberdashers' Monmouth School for Girls,
Monmouth

Fight or Flight

by Alice Mainstone

I don't know whose fault she thought it was, but it definitely wasn't mine. We stared down at the cat – what had been the cat – unable to look away. I knew that she was waiting for me to look away. She would take my inability to look at the sad, broken shape on the road as an admission of guilt, a weakness that she could attack mercilessly until I would feel like the small creature destroyed by the uncaring, unmarked machine.

She would speak first, as always, and state her case, attack me before I had even thought of a defence... but not yet. She was gathering up her anger, turning it over and over in her heart while her head struggled to contain it in words. She would sharpen them until they were as cutting as a sword, then she'd take her swing at me. And my armour was dented enough already.

This was only the calm before the storm, the still water that hides a vicious current. The silence was beating in my ears, and even the wind paused its howling, realising it could not compete with what was coming.

'I can't believe you did that,' she said, very

quietly. The silence seemed to intensify. 'I can't BELIEVE you did that.'

I stayed silent, waiting for my sentence to fall.

'As if you hadn't ruined my evening enough already? Did you think it would be funny? Or did you just want to shock me?' She didn't wait for an answer before continuing. 'You just didn't think, did you. You never just stop and think.'

In my head I grabbed her by the collar of that slightly too-tight dress and shook her until her stiff hair fell out of place and that sneer slid off her face. In my head she sighs and tells me she's sorry and she loves me so very much. Each image is as satisfying as the other, and just as unlikely. I was still staring at the dead cat as she went on.

'You could never drive. Another thing you're useless at. I would have seen it. This is the last time I let you drive me anywhere. Next time you'll hit a person and when you get locked up I won't come and visit.'

She was slurring her words now as she talked about how careless I was. I felt my muscles tense and my hands clench into fists. I remembered someone telling me once about adrenaline, and how the rush is designed to enable fight or flight for survival. I had never felt enough fear or anger to do either, but now I felt hot fury blazing inside me as she repeated her list of complaints against me.

'Maybe,' I interrupted, 'if you hadn't drunk

so much you could have driven. But no doubt you would have found something else to complain about.'

I could feel her eyes on me and finally I looked up from the cat. Her mouth was open in an unattractive parody of surprise, her eyes slightly unfocused as she took an unsteady step towards me. 'What did you just say to me?'

I knew she had heard me by the disbelief in her voice. The cat was quite forgotten now, its temporary mourners had moved on. It lay between us and the car, still and silent, and in that moment I envied it. The flash of headlights, a quick bump and that had been it. It seemed our end would be far more drawn out and painful as we negotiated blame. I felt a sudden need to prove my innocence in the cat's death.

'It was dark. Stupid thing shouldn't have been on the road,' I muttered.

'You should have seen it!' she shouted, though I knew the cat's death was not what was making her angry.

'Maybe if you had just let me drive and not given me a blow by blow account of all my mistakes this evening then I would have,' I snapped back.

'Well someone had to tell you what a fool you make of yourself! Every single time....'

She continued to shout at me, though I seemed to be drifting away. The cat still lay there, spilling its secrets to the night while we screamed our troubles for anyone to hear. I thought back to that moment when that streak of yellow dashed out into the road and that sickening thud as we hit it. I had looked over at her, hardly caring if she was all right. Her face, usually controlled, was blank. Her eyes wide and unseeing and her face pale. She had looked so vulnerable. She had turned to me and I'd expected her to ask for comfort, reassurance, I had wanted her to so badly. But she'd looked away from me and gotten out of the car.

Hardly realising what I was doing, I walked past the body of the cat toward the car.

'What are you doing?' she screamed at me. 'Don't just think we can get back in the car and that'll be the end of it.'

I turned and faced her. She looked startled, and I can only imagine my outward appearance reflected the battle inside me and it scared her. 'I am getting back in the car, and I am leaving, and that will be the end of it. This is the end of it.'

She caught hold of my arm, though I hardly noticed. 'You can't just leave,' she said, her voice shaking. 'What about....'

In the second that she paused our eyes met. I waited for her to beg me not to go, for her to apologise, just for her to ask me to care about her.

'What about the cat?' she finished quietly.

'The cat?'

'Shouldn't we call a vet or something? They might still be able to do something.'

I looked at her incredulously. 'Some things can't be fixed,' I replied, 'even if you want them to be.'

As I drove away I looked back and saw her staring after me. She looked so lost and alone I almost turned back. Then I remembered. Fight or flight. Today I chose flight.

By Alice Mainstone, aged 17
Knox Academy, East Lothian

'It was a Peruvian blue-finned piranha, one of the rarest and most dangerous fish in the world. But what was it doing in my bath?'

Philip Reeve

Fish Story

by Pandora Dewan

It was a Peruvian blue-finned piranha, one of the rarest and most dangerous fish in the world. But what was it doing in my bath? I was staying at my granddad's house for a week. It was nowhere near to Peru, one of those old New England houses which have a musty smell, and curiosity lurking in the air.

Granddad had told me to run a quick bath before the White Willow Hotel party that evening. I turned on the bath and went downstairs to feed the dog. When I got back I saw the fish.

I stood there in awe. This would be one swell story to tell my friends back in Hedgegroves, my home village. The piranha was snapping at me, sending foamy bubbles and water across the tiles. One thing was certain. I wasn't getting in that bath.

I ran downstairs to tell my grandfather about the piranha. I wasn't sure he would believe me, but instead he jumped up from the sofa and commanded me to show him.

I might as well tell you now that my granddad isn't just any granddad. He is a wizard.

Indeed he is Head Startremium, the chief constable of magic in our world.

'That one was meant for me,' sighed my granddad. 'I'm glad you had the sense not to go in there. How on earth did you know that it was a piranha?'

I held out my copy of *Dreamers of the Deep Guide*. 'I've always been interested in piranhas,' I said. 'It seems to me that if I could tame one then it would be a good pet. Sort of like a guard dog underwater.'

'Silly boy!' said my granddad. 'Very dangerous creatures!'

I felt ashamed.

'OK then, stand back.' Granddad cleared his throat and conjured a spell. POOF! Smoke and red sparks filled the room, but when we looked back at the bath... 'That wasn't supposed to happen,' said Granddad.

The fish was twice the size, and more violent then ever. It was a magic fish, and every time magic was used on it, it grew.

Granddad called up his friend, Eliot Eelwart, head of the Depthanium Division.

'Can it wait for the morning?' asked Eliot.

'No! It's starting to steam,' Granddad said.

'Can you get it down to the hotel tonight?'

Granddad thought he could.

'Well then put it in the fountain at 8:00 tonight, I'll be down to it at the first free moment I get. I should be able to slip away for about ten minutes at that time.'

Obviously, Granddad couldn't use any more magic, but I'm good with animals, so somehow we captured it in a large plastic cookie box. I carried it on my knee in the car, as Granddad drove at breakneck speed. The thing sloshed about. I prayed it didn't eat plastic.

There was the hotel. We dashed out of the car and released the piranha into the fountain. Just at that moment I thought I saw a camera flash from the balcony above, but Granddad had already rushed off to find Eliot.

Something bothered me about that flash. I looked at the reflection in the water and calculated where that window would be. Something told me not to look round. I went into the hotel. I reckoned that balcony had to be on the second floor. I had to find out more, so I stepped into the elevator. The doors opened on the second floor. Around the corner I could hear someone talking. My instinct told me it would be better not to be seen. I hid in the cupboard on the landing. My instinct was right.

'Where'd the kid go?' whispered one.

'Never mind the kid, he can be dealt with later. Important thing is we've photographed Boss Man chucking a piranha into the fountain just before the children dance in there. Won't Eliot be pleased.'

The kid they were talking about had to be me, which meant that Boss Man was my granddad. He was being framed! I had to get to Granddad, but first I had to get that piranha out of that fountain.

I rushed back down to the fountain. Trying not to look suspicious I knelt down on the edge to look for the piranha. Suddenly some ice-cold hands pushed me into the water. I panicked. I was swimming with a piranha! I caught sight of it heading towards me. It drew nearer, snapping its hungry jaws. Clearly I was on its dinner menu.

I was pretty desperate. 'No. Please!' I gurgled, 'I'm begging you! Stop! I bet you're a nice piranha really! You wouldn't like the taste of me, I might be poisonous!'

But why would a piranha listen? I was certain it would bite a chunk out of me. I was ready to feel its dagger teeth any second... but instead the most peculiar thing happened. The piranha slowed down. It looked at me with its red button fishy eyes. Then it spoke.

'What?' it asked. It really had talked.

'Please stop,' I gasped.

'Alright, I will. You're the first human who has ever spoken to me. I respect you.'

And that's when I discovered my gift of talking to animals.

When I rose up from the water there was a crowd of people staring into the fountain

'How did you survive?' someone asked.

'Is it gone?'

'Did you kill it?'

'Will it hurt my baby?'

As if I wasn't wet enough I was showered with questions.

Another person shouted, 'The evil chief constable has thrown you into the fountain with the piranha he put in. We saw the photo! We've called the police to come and get him.'

I was worried. Granddad was going to be arrested. I scanned the huge clump of people until I saw Eliot and his men.

'My granddad is not the culprit of this crime,' I yelled, and pointed at Eliot. 'He is.'

Eliot looked up and then made a run for it, but he was too late. People barred the exits. Eliot was trapped and my granddad was safe.

When the police arrived they asked if there was anything they could do to repay me. I thought, and then I said, 'Well, do you think I can, um, keep that piranha as a pet? We kinda bonded.'

Granddad groaned, but I was the one who saved the day so they let me keep the piranha. His name is Binky. He is swimming in his bowl right next to me, helping me write this.

Pandora Dewan, aged 11
Oxford High School

The Light of Uluru

by Alistair Brown

It was a Peruvian blue-finned piranha, one of the rarest and more dangerous fish in the world. But what was it doing in my bath? I gazed, transfixed, as it swam gracefully around the bathtub for a while. Then, before my eyes, it began to flicker and seem to change form, and, after a few seconds I was looking at a fully-grown Inca man.

With my mind reeling and head pounding from the shock, I simply sprinted out of the bathroom, slammed the door shut and wedged it with a chair. For a few minutes, I stood with my back against the wall, breathing heavily, trying to get my head around what had just happened. Eventually I decided that the man was a burglar who was trying to trick me with visual illusions. All I had to do to get rid of him was to phone the police. Several phone calls and sceptical policemen later, I was told that someone would be sent round.

*   *   *

After half an hour of tedious waiting, I was coldly greeted at the door by a stern-looking policewoman, who demanded to be shown to the area where I had 'apprehended the thief'. Resisting the urge to argue against her sarcastic tone, I dutifully led her to the bathroom, where we found the man, sitting in the bath, reading the Daily Mirror. Quickly recovering from the surprise, the stunned officer stepped forward and ordered him to stand up and put his hands behind his head. At this point, he glanced up to her with an uninterested look, which quickly changed to pleased and whispered, 'Ah, this was meant to be.'

Drawing out a pair of handcuffs, the policewoman repeated her order. With an amused expression on his face, the man simply looked at her for a few seconds, then flickered, and turned back into the fish.

Even this stony-faced, austere policewoman was not prepared for this. She staggered backwards, knocking all the deodorants, toothbrushes and toothpaste off the side with her flailing arms. Slipping on the floor, she fell back and grazed her hands on the red, dusty, rock. Rock?

My heart seemed to stop. On all sides I was surrounded by dry grasslands, with the hot Australian sun beating down on my neck. In the distance, a kookaburra called out. I was on top of Ayers Rock. It was too much to take in, and the last thing I remembered before passing out was the figure of the man, standing, god-like, on the plateau of rock.

*   *   *

By the time I woke, stars were twinkling above me and a cool breeze was blowing. I sat up slowly, and saw, by a glowing fire, the policewoman and the Inca, seemingly aged by the firelight. Without looking, he beckoned for me to join them.

Obediently, I did as he asked, and moved over to the toasty, crackling fire.

'I'm sorry,' he began, with his ancient voice. 'This must have been a terrifying ordeal for both of you.' He paused, as if unsure of what to say next. 'I don't know where to begin with what I'm about to tell you,' he continued, 'so I'll start with the facts. The world is ending. The fabric of space is being ripped apart and creating wormholes, like the one between your bathroom and Uluru. A hole opened and we dropped through like a stone in a wet paper bag.'

An image of a robot flashed up in my head saying the same thing but with the added, 'I hate wet paper bags.' It seemed impossible that anything as ordinary as radio shows and Marvin the Paranoid Android could ever have taken place. They seemed so long ago. I snapped back to the present, eager to hear more of what the man had to say.

'The force that holds us together is failing,' droned the man, 'allowing us to change shape at will. A long time ago, my people realised that this was going to happen. It had taken place before, humanity destroyed, two left to begin the cycle again.

'When the invaders, the conquistadors, arrived, we tried to warn them. But they didn't listen. They burned down our temples and smashed our calendars. Only a few survived, but they were enough to give them an idea of what was coming. You know, I'm sure, of the 2012 prediction?'

I nodded mutely.

'Good. It was a true doom though, not just a crazed fantasy. After a time, we realized that our efforts to warn them were futile, and set off across the sea to our brothers in Oceania. There was no need to enlighten them. They had come to the same conclusion and built, like our temples, a monument in the hope that it would protect them against what was to come. For them, the protection was to look natural, so they laboured for decades, but it paid off. For when they were finished, it was a magnificent wonder. Greater than the creations of all who sought to slow the fury of ending. Greater than Stonehenge, the pyramids or any other. They built Uluru. Settlers arrived here too though, so we went into hiding. And so we have remained, reading the stars, waiting for the two to be born. Until now.'

As he ended, the sun rose. The sun of the 21st of December 2012. With it came a great host of people; Inca, Aztec, Aborigine and many other supposedly finished civilisations. Our friend went down to join them and, as one they surrounded the rock and began a low, quiet chant. The light got brighter, and I saw that it came not from the Sun, but from under the Earth. The Light of Ending rose from under the crust of the Earth and consumed all. When it cleared, all that was left was a man and a woman on top of a rock.

And the cycle began again.

Alistair Brown, aged 14
Gartree High School, Leicestershire

'I'm sorry,' Mum said. 'But I've got no choice and you never know, boarding school might be fun.'

Sarah Webb

The Chair

by Rachel Knott

'I'm sorry,' Mum said. 'But I've got no choice and you never know, boarding school might be fun.' Voice a tremulous squeak; she sat in her chair – overlong fingernails digging into the arms of her favourite armchair. Once a vibrant butter yellow, it now sat threadbare and faded in front of the large bay window. She smiled weakly, eyes alight and wild.

I played along. 'Oh, like in an Enid Blyton novel?'

'Yes,' she whispered, leaning forward with enthusiasm. I could see the outline of her collarbone through her cardigan. 'Yes, yes. Enid Blyton, oh wonderful!'

We'd read all the Malory Towers the past winter. The weeks there hadn't been money for the electric bill; her in the worn yellow armchair as I read aloud. We'd used candles, sometimes she'd joke that it was romantic. They'd been cheap; the smell as they burnt was awful. Acrid. I'd wince every time I lit one. She sat, wrapped in blankets. Small and frail, like a little bird. Some nights she would fall asleep after a few pages, paper-thin eyelids fluttering as she dreamt. Other times we'd stay up until the early hours and my voice got hoarse so the words came out in tired scratches.

'With the uniform,' she added. 'Yellow, like sunshine. To match your hair,' she smiled, the corners of her eyes crinkling.

'But won't you miss me?' I said in a singsong voice, the way she liked me to.

'Of course, of course. I'll miss you, of course. But you'll make so many friends.' She let out a small contented sigh. 'Yes, so many friends.' She pulled the cardigan tighter toward herself, craning to stare out of the window. Outside, to the fading amber sky, as the sun drew lower overhead. The street was empty. Twisting her fingers about the buttons, soft, pink mother of pearl, she watched, eyes trained on the streetlights. I sat. Her hair, thin and broken in a pile atop her head, shone red in the late afternoon light. When the first lamp flickered on, she cooed quietly to herself.

'I had so many friends,' she murmured, eyes never leaving the orange glow of the streetlight. 'We had such fun together.' Her voice trailed off, hands falling into her lap, leaving the buttons of her cardigan mismatched and undone. Narrow and delicate, veins like tiny blue rivers. She had been able to fasten the tiniest of clasps until her eyesight became poor and she strained to see. The most intricate catch, every dainty doll's accessory, I had brought them all to her. To sit and watch as she worked with those slight fingers, so long and graceful in their movements.

'There, all done,' she would say, her face creased in a bright smile.

Hands in the folds of the blanket as the last day's light shone in through the window, she blinked, slow and laboured, long pale lashes brushing against the soft skin of her cheek.

'Bring me the album,' she said, raising her arms; pointing. 'The album, bring it to me.'

I stood. The springs of the sofa let out a lazy groan as they unwound. Crossing the room, I peered in the dim light, reaching out as I neared the bookcase. My fingers brushed over rigid hardback, well-thumbed novels with broken spines and faded covers. I stopped as I felt buttery leather beneath my fingertips, comforting like an old friend. Picking it up off the shelf, I rubbed my thumb across its worn edges, remembering every line and wrinkle.

She held out her hand, taking it from me to nestle in her lap. The pages were yellowing, growing thin and curled at the edges with passing years. The corners of her mouth quirked as she smoothed out the paper, tracing the faces that smiled back at her, caught forever in some long forgotten moment.

'Mmm,' she hummed. 'We were so young, so pretty. All those smiles... such laughter. Lovely, lovely.'

'Which one are you?' I asked, leaning closer as if to search for her face though I knew which happy laughing girl she was.

'There,' she pointed. 'Second row, third from the right. With my hair in curls. I had such wonderful hair, everyone always said. Such wonderful hair.'

The face, eyes full of mirth, gazed back at me. Full, high cheekbones, pinched blazing pink as her mouth parted in a smile. She looked young, happy. Squinting, I looked, as I always did, for some semblance of the shrunken woman in the chair before me. Only her eyes, bright cerulean blue, gave her away. When I was small, I would sit with the album laid out on the floor, trying to imagine my mother so vibrant as she appeared on paper. The laughing girl in the sweater and the soft-spoken woman I knew seemed two entirely separate entities. Often, I had wondered whether it was another of her fantasies, a game she played to pass the time.

'I'm tired,' she mumbled, pushing away the album. It fell to the floor, lying face down into the patterned rug. 'I want to sleep.'

I picked up the leather-bound book and placed it back on the table beside her chair. With one last look outside, I shut the curtains on the bright shining moon. Fumbling, she turned on the lamp, casting an orange warmth over the room. I bent to tuck the blankets around her, wrapped in their safe embrace. She reached for my cheek and pressed her lips to it, softly. I could smell her scent; clean and comforting. Drawing back, she dropped her hand and settled back into the chair, like a baby bird in its nest.

'You're a good girl,' she whispered. 'I have no choice, I'm sorry.'

'I know,' I said soothingly, smoothing over her blankets with a gentle hand. 'I know, it's okay.'

She nodded, slowly shutting her eyes. 'You'll have so much fun,' she rasped. 'So many friends....'

I backed out of the room, pausing at the door to watch a moment as her small chest rose and fell with each heavy breath. She never looked so small as she did in that chair, hunched like a woman twice her age, her translucent skin amplified by the lamplight. Her hands lay clasped together in her lap, fingers once so slender now gnarled like tree roots. She sat motionless, only murmuring softly to herself, silent games that even I couldn't play along with.

'I'll pack my case tonight,' I said to no one but myself; the words she liked me to say. 'Nice and neat.'

With a last glance back to her tiny frame in the tired old chair, I pulled the door shut behind me. Listening, as I always did, for that distinctive *click* as it closed before walking up the hallway to my room, in the dark.

Rachel Knott, aged 17
Kesgrave High School, Suffolk

The Boarding School Time Slip

by Alexander Bowes

'I'm sorry,' Mum said. 'But I've got no choice and you never know, boarding school might be fun.'

'No way! Not if you're being sent back in time to some boarding school that you've never heard of to get experience in how things were done in those times. I could end up anywhere,' protested John.

'We have to do as the council of elders instructs us to do,' insisted Mum.

'Some encouraging, supportive mum you are; and I wish that I wasn't the son of a time traveller so that I could go to normal schools and stay there.'

'The fact remains that when you wake up tomorrow morning... you won't be... (how can I put it?) at home,' said Mum nervously.

'I hate being the son of a time lord,' John muttered.

The next morning, when John woke up, instead of seeing the bright blue rock star wallpaper in his bedroom, he saw every imaginable shade of green. He could smell the scents of the trees and he felt a light, delicate wind on his face. The sun was blazing like a motionless burning star. Instead of the relentless, high-pitched 'get up' from Mum, he heard a deep booming sound like a giant stomping downstairs when he had just been woken up. As he slowly gathered his bearings he made out what the voice was saying: 'Get up you lazy fool.'

Same words, wrong voice, John thought.

John quickly realised that he had ended up in a Spartan school which was situated in woods and a series of caves in the mountains surrounding Sparta. He vaguely remembered learning about them in a history class last year. He recalled that the Spartans were a fierce, proud, warlike people who took boys from their parents when they were only seven years old so that they could be trained to be warriors. John, however, was ten and had a lot of catching up to do. Although he was a black belt in martial arts in the year 2064, he had never been trained to wear armour and use the weapons the Spartans used.

John heard a loud, war cry and when he looked up he saw a young boy with a dagger running at him ferociously. His lightning sharp reflexes enabled him to dodge the dagger, strike and punch the boy in the temple, knocking him flat out.

'Good,' boomed the instructor, 'but how will you cope when you are situated on the front lines against some bloody Persian army, eh?'

As what felt like seven years went by, John learnt how to use weapons such as the dorine (a spear with a tip at the top and at the bottom to balance it, the bottom tip was also used as a spare weapon). Unfortunately for him, he had scars on his back and he had injured several men just because they wanted to see how he would cope in the front lines. He had made friends with one or two of the other boys even though friendship was not encouraged as it was considered to be sign of weakness. Now, he was about to face his last challenge in order to become a Spartan warrior, he would have to kill an unarmed peasant, and not get caught doing it….

That night, as he approached a small isolated village, he smiled as the only person to be seen was a slave, working in a courtyard. John studied the man's build, very skinny, he thought, probably starved. He was wearing a torn ragged tunic; his sandals were rather like leather pieces strapped around his foot, blowing delicately in the sleek autumn breeze. He was smiling to himself, it seemed he was starved of independence and filled with loneliness, and was gratefully welcoming the emotion. A beaming star was his face, glowing like a child on Christmas morning. As he brushed away the leaves, beaming at the immaculate courtyard he had tidied, he noticed a small movement in the trees.

'Never mind,' John heard him say. 'Probably just the wind, or me losing my mind so I must not allow the natural earth to play tricks on me.'

Maybe something had gone wrong when he had travelled through time or was John simply being taught a lesson about how civilized school was in the year 2064? After all, he had been a difficult, lazy and disruptive student at his previous school. John sat down and tried to reflect on what seemed to be a very long journey, he had been sent back in time, taught how to steal, fight, kill, invade and command. He could not prevent a tear from trickling down his smooth cheek.

'Why all this suffering, do they believe this is how children should be raised, do they think this is setting an example?' John muttered to himself whilst he started to cry. 'That slave is innocent; he has spent all his life being treated as if he is dirt in the world. And I take for granted the fact that I was born in a wealthy time lord family, important politically and socially. No matter how tough and flamboyant I try to be, it just doesn't feel right. At home I am well mannered and polite – perhaps I should be like that at school. What were those martial arts saying again? Treat others the way that you want to be treated. Yes. It's clear to me now,' and then a voice in his head interrupted him saying:

'Get on with the horrible deed will you, it's almost dawn!'

'Yes, yes, I will.' Reluctantly he got up and crouched on his feet, he smoothly and quickly slid behind one of the tavernas (a Greek restaurant).

As he went in for the kill, he realized he had no weapons with him.

'Blast.'

'What! Who's there?' shouted the startled slave as he turned around. 'Who are you, MASTER, a guest?'

'No I've failed, you little....'

But before he could finish, he heard the distinctive sound of his dad. 'Don't bother, John, you don't have to do this! There was a problem, you weren't supposed to be here so come home with me.'

'I... I can't, I belong here, friendship is pain,' John muttered.

'You know that's not true, you are not like that John, you are warm-hearted boy, not a killing machine. Come home now.'

As John turned around to face his dad, he knew that he was wrong, and should have listened. 'Alright Dad, I'll come.'

But as they walked away, they heard the slave muttering, 'You?... time lord... what?... that, uh life is **confusing**.' And with that the slave fainted.

'Come on boy,' said Dad, 'let's go home. No more boarding schools for you.'

Alexander Bowes, aged 11
Bournemouth School

<u>Heroes</u>

'When I am old and looking back
Who will the heroes be?
What deeds will they have done?'

Roger McGough

Heroes

by Mathilde Rimbert

When I am old and looking back
Who will the heroes be?
What deeds will they have done?
What changes will we see?

The knight in shining armour
Rescuing the princess in her tower,
Firemen fighting a sea of flames
Were the heroes of my earliest hour.

Rock stars singing lyrics to a crowd,
Models strolling down runways,
Handsome Hollywood actors
Make up the heroes of my teenage days.

Freedom fighters and peacemakers
Never ceasing in their strife,
Statesmen with soul-stirring speeches
Compose the heroes of my adult life.

When I am old and grey with years,
Will Earth be left to save?
Will there be a place for heroes
Will there still be a home for the brave?

Mathilde Rimbert, aged 14
College Pierre et Marie Curie, France

Heroes

by Joe Cooper

When I am old and looking back
Who will the heroes be?
What deeds will they have done?
Could it be you or me?
Did they save the world from aliens
Or try to make world peace,
Save humanity from extinction
Or help confused police?

But can one man stand against an army,
To unite two warring states,
Cut short global warming
Or move tectonic plates?
Not one of us can stand alone,
But if their cause is sound,
We will rally to their banner
Until the truth is found.

Inside every one of us,
Part of a hero lies,
And when we stand together,
Under harsh, uncaring skies,
Our voices will be heard by all,
As the inner hero stirs,
With power to move mountains
And fight for many years.

So when I'm old and looking back,
Thinking who the heroes were,
It will be every one of us
Who stood for what was true and fair.
When *you're* thinking of the future,
What heroes there will be,
Just say quietly to yourself,
'That hero could be me.'

Joe Cooper, aged 15
Hethersett High School, Norwich

Notes